ROB CHILDS

COUNTY CUP

Book Two
The East Quarter

Cup Rivals

Illustrated by Robin Lawrie

CORGI YEARLING BOOKS

J91,899
£3-99

CUP RIVALS
A CORGI YEARLING BOOK : 0 440 863848

First publication in Great Britain

PRINTING HISTORY
Corgi Yearling edition published 2000

1 3 5 7 9 10 8 6 4 2

Set in 12/15 pt New Century Schoolbook by
Phoenix Typesetting, Ilkley, West Yorkshire

Corgi Yearling Books are published by Transworld Publishers,
61-63 Uxbridge Road, London W5 5SA,
a division of The Random House Group Ltd,
in Australia by Random House Australia (Pty) Ltd,
20 Alfred Street, Milsons Point, Sydney, NSW 2061, Australia,
in New Zealand by Random House New Zealand Ltd,
18 Poland Road, Glenfield, Auckland 10, New Zealand
and in South Africa by Random House (Pty) Ltd,
Endulini, 5a Jubilee Road, Parktown 2193, South Africa

Made and printed in Great Britain by
Cox & Wyman Ltd, Reading, Berkshire

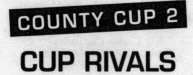

COUNTY CUP 2

CUP RIVALS

INTRODUCTION

L ong ago, the historic county of Medland was made up of four separate regions. These divisions can now only be found on ancient maps, but people living in the old North, South, East and West Quarters still remain loyal to their own area.

One way that the traditional rivalry between the Quarters is kept up is by means of the County Cup.

Every year, schools from all over the county take part in this great soccer tournament and the standard of football is always high. Matches are played on a local group basis at first to decide the Quarter Champions, who will then clash in the knockout stages of the competition later in the season.

The winners receive the much-prized silver trophy and earn the right to call themselves the County Champions – the top team in Medland.

THE COUNTY OF MEDLAND

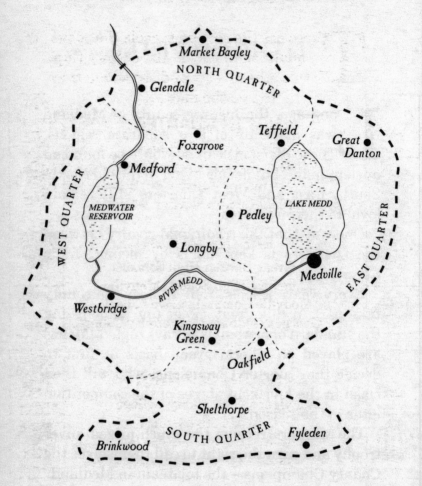

Market Bagley

NORTH QUARTER

Glendale

Teffield

Great Danton

Foxgrove

WEST QUARTER

Medford

MEDWATER RESERVOIR

LAKE MEDD

Pedley

EAST QUARTER

Longby

Medville

RIVER MEDD

Westbridge

Kingsway Green

Oakfield

Shelthorpe

Fyleden

Brinkwood

SOUTH QUARTER

SCHOOLS

These are the sixteen schools that have qualified to play in the County Cup this season – try and see where they are on the map . . .

NORTH QUARTER

Foxgrove High School
Glendale Community School
Market Bagley Community School
Teffield Comprehensive School

EAST QUARTER

Great Danton High School
Lakeview High School, Medville
Medville Comprehensive School
Sir George Needham Community College,
Pedley

SOUTH QUARTER

Fyleden Community College
Oakfield High School
Shelthorpe Comprehensive School
St Wystan's Comprehensive School,
Brinkwood

WEST QUARTER

Hillcrest Comprehensive School, Longby
Kingsway Green High School
Riverside Comprehensive School, Medford
Westbridge Community College

Labwin High School.

a Great Danton High School

Sir George Markham Community College

Midville Comprehensive School

MEET THE TEAMS

Saturday 11 October is an important date for many young footballers in the East Quarter of Medland. That's when the County Cup competition will kick off in their area. Each of the four schools involved will be hoping to be crowned Quarter Champions by the end of term.

The opening fixtures in the round-robin group are:

> Great Danton High School v
> Lakeview High School
>
> Medville Comprehensive School v
> Sir George Needham Community College

Meet the teams on the next few pages and perhaps even choose one that you might like to support in their games. Then follow their fortunes in this book to see what happens in the exciting quest for the County Cup.

Who will be Champions of the East?

Read on and find out . . .

GREAT DANTON HIGH SCHOOL

Small high school in the village of Great Danton near the eastern boundary of Medland, with pupils in year groups 7, 8 and 9 only, aged between 11 and 14.

Headteacher: *Mrs Elizabeth Ruskin*

Teacher in charge of year 7 soccer: *Mr Bill Goddard*

School colours: *red and white striped shirts, red shorts and socks*

Year 7 soccer captain: *Chris Vaughan*

Usual team formation: *4–4–2*

Year 7 soccer squad:

Nidesh Pandya

(Woody)
Brian Woods   Matthew Lee   James O'Neill   Chris Vaughan

Daniel Cooper   Josh Wintour   Luke Munton   Alex Lloyd

Adam Quinn   Sam Isherwood (Ishy)
(Q)

plus: Gopal Desai, Trevor Priest, Jack Roberts, Sam Lawson, Joe Morrison

CAPTAIN'S Notes...

Meet the God Squad — that's what we like to call ourselves, after our teacher Mr Goddard. It's not that we want to rely on the power of prayer to help us win the County Cup, but at least we can always ask a Priest — Trevor, that is — to say one for us if we're ever in trouble!

We'd rather rely on the scoring powers of our twin strikers, Q and Ishy, and we like to think our defence isn't bad either. It's been strengthened by the addition of Nidesh in goal and also Woody, who both went to primary schools in other Quarters of Medland.

I'm the only natural left-footed player in the God Squad, so we might lack a bit of balance, but a few others can use their left OK when they have to. The big schools from Medville are probably favourites in our group, but don't rule us out. They won't find us a pushover — especially when we have divine guidance on our side!

LAKEVIEW HIGH SCHOOL

Medium-sized secondary school in the county town of Medville in the East Quarter, overlooking Lake Medd. Pupils in year groups 7, 8 and 9 only, aged between 11 and 14.

Headteacher: *Mr John Underwood*
P.E. teacher: *Miss Ruth Jackson*
School colours: *blue shirts, white shorts and socks*
Year 7 soccer captain: *Ben Thorpe*
Usual team formation: *3–5–2*

Year 7 soccer squad:

Michael King (Elvis)

James Black   Andy Peacock   Will Freeman

Joe Vernon   Dan Maynard

Steve Jarvis   Ben Thorpe   Ian Coates

Matthew Tudor   Ravi Mistry
(Henry)

plus: Gary (Gordon) Bennett, Manjit Bedi, Jaspal Singh, Thomas Farr, Alan Davis, Nathan Finch

CAPTAIN'S
Notes...

We're not quite sure what to expect this season at our new school as the Year 7 soccer team is run by a female teacher, Miss Jackson. At least she always knocks on the door before coming into our changing room!

Jacko plays the game herself for Medville Ladies and has also been capped at county level so she must be pretty good. Have to go and watch her in action sometime.

Here's a quick namecheck for you on a few of the players. I'm Ben in midfield and my best mate is Elvis — the King — in goal. Jacko wants to use wing-backs, so it looks like Joe and Dan will do that job as they've both got the stamina to bomb up and down the pitch all match. Henry and Ravi were picked up front for our first league game — we won 3—1 — but they'll have to keep banging the ball in the net to hold their places as we've got some good strikers in the squad. Should be an interesting season . . .

L arge comprehensive school in the county town of Medville in the East Quarter.

Headteacher: *Mr Alan Fuller*
P.E. teacher: *Mr Steve Yardley*
School colours: *all-red*
Year 7 soccer captain: *Ryan Burns*
Usual team formation: 4–3–3

Year 7 soccer squad:

Ryan Burns

(Skinny)
Matthew Twigg   Sam Kitson   Afzal Malik   David Ball

(Monty)
Satish Gupte   Mark Emerson   Jack Montgomery

Robin Yorke   Adam Bridges   Scott Joyner

plus: Anil Shah, Josh Manchester (United), Paramjit Maan (Pram-Man), Phil Carter, Harry Glenn, George Bingham, Aaron Statham

CAPTAIN'S Notes...

I'm Ryan Burns, keeper and captain of Medville Comp, the best team in town. We aim to prove we're the best in the East Quarter as well and then the best in the whole of Medland by winning the County Cup.

Our main rivals will be Lakeview High on the other side of town, but we don't rate them all that much. We can't wait to thrash them in our local Derbies in league and cup games.

Six players in our squad represented the area team last season at primary level. That's me in goal of course, plus defenders Skinny and Sam, Monty in midfield, and Adam and Scott in attack. A few of the others went to the area trials too so you can see we've got a dead strong squad. Can't see how anybody can stand in our way of going one better than last year's Comp team which lost in the County Final.

Make sure you support us. You don't want to be losers, do you?

Large secondary school in the town of Pedley in the East Quarter.

Principal: *Dr Colin Chisholm*

Teacher in charge of Year 7 football: *Mr Fraser O'Donald*

School colours: *white shirts, black shorts and socks*

Year 7 football captain: *Jayesh Parmar*

Usual team formation: *4–2–4*

Year 7 football squad:

David Williams (D.J)

Mark Jewell   Barry Hope   Callum Haynes   David Williams (Dazza)

Richard Simmons   Karl Zaturowski (Zat)

Kyle Baker   Jayesh Parmar (Jay)   Tom Wright   Paul Allen

plus: Floyd Austin, Ian Dawson, Philip Cork (Champagne), Jason Thatcher, Stuart Owen, Jeff Edmonds

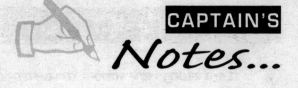

CAPTAIN'S Notes...

I am very proud to be the first Asian pupil to have the honour of being captain of the College football team. The College has a long history, founded by Sir George Needham in the nineteenth century, but this is the first time that it has qualified to take part in the County Cup.

Notice that we always call it football here. The College Principal, Dr Chisholm, does not like us using the word soccer.

Let me introduce you to some of the squad. We play with two wingers, Kyle and Paul, and we also have two players with the same name, David Williams. To avoid confusion, the goalkeeper is known by two of his initials, D.J., and the full-back is Dazza. Watch out for another defender, Callum, storming upfield to join in the attack, especially at set-pieces. He is brilliant in the air.

I hope that you will come and cheer on the College.

LAKE MEDD

. . . it's Friday afternoon and two boys are standing on the southern shore of Lake Medd, skimming stones across the surface of the water. The cousins are wearing different school uniforms . . .

'Wow! See that one?' cried Joe. 'Must've been at least a tenner!'

Harry sneered. 'No way! Six or seven at the most. Don't they teach you to count at Lakeview?'

'Better than at the Comp obviously. At least we can count up to ten.'

Harry's next effort sank after only three skips.

'What a failure!' Joe scoffed.

'Can't find any good flat stones round here.'

'Excuses, excuses! You'll have to come up with some better ones than that when we slaughter the Comp in the Cup.'

'No need,' Harry sighed. 'I don't reckon I'll be playing.'

'How d'yer know that? You're in their squad, aren't you?'

'Well, I go to the practices, if that's what you mean. I haven't even been picked as sub yet.'

'Early doors,' Joe said mischievously, knowing such football slang always irritated Harry. 'The season's hardly started.'

Harry slumped against a wall and kicked his bulging school bag a few times with the toe of his left shoe. It was badly scuffed after the lunchtime kickabout in the playground. His right was unmarked.

'I think the only door I'll be seeing is the one marked Exit.'

'C'mon, cheer up. It's the weekend.'

'Yeah, and just look at the size of this bag. I've got tons of homework to do. Where's yours, by the way?'

'Left it at school. Nobody gave us any work.'

'Lucky thing,' Harry grunted, giving his bag an extra hard thump.

'They know we've got more important things to do this weekend. It's the County Cup tomorrow.'

'Not for me, it isn't.'

'Sorry – forgot. Are you going to watch the Comp play?'

Harry shook his head. 'I'd rather stay in bed.'

'Lazybones! Why don't you come and watch me instead? Dad'll give you a lift with us.'

'Might do. I'll think about it.'

Joe selected another stone and crouched to sling it across the water. He got the angle all wrong this time and the stone nosedived into the lake.

'Hey, brilliant!' laughed Harry. 'What's *your* excuse for that one?'

Joe grinned sheepishly. 'No excuse. I'm just as sick as a parrot!'

. . . right, time for some soccer action. Let's see if Joe's aim is any better in the morning when Lakeview travel to meet Great Danton . . .

GREAT DANTON v LAKEVIEW

Saturday 11 October
k.o. 10 a.m.
Referee: Mr B. Goddard

... after a goal-less first half, Harry is wondering whether it was worth getting out of bed to come and watch – then his cousin wakes the game up ...

'Yes, Elvis – I'm in space.'

The Lakeview goalkeeper responded to the shout by hurling the ball out towards his right wing-back. The throw was a little wayward and put Joe under unnecessary pressure.

'Man on!' Elvis cried.

Joe already knew that. He'd had to move swiftly to win the ball and suffered a kick on the ankle for his pains. The opponent continued to hassle him as Joe shielded the ball with his body until he managed to wriggle free. At least he thought so, but he was soon yanked back by the shirt.

The whistle blew. 'Free-kick to Blues,' said the referee.

'No need to try and swap shirts,' said Joe crossly as the boy ran off to mark someone else.

Joe stabbed the free-kick to a teammate in the centre-circle and set off up the wing, calling for a return pass. As he regained possession, another barrier to his progress loomed up in the shape of the Great Danton captain. Joe knew from previous tussles that there was no point in trying to beat him for speed so he simply took a big swipe at the ball instead.

It was intended more as a centre than a shot at goal, but the wind caught the ball in flight and it swirled wickedly through the air. The Danton goalkeeper was taken totally by surprise. Nidesh failed to get his hands anywhere near the ball and it smacked against the crossbar like a thunderclap.

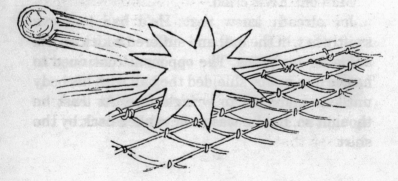

Nor did he have any chance to recover in time to deal with the rebound. The ball landed kindly at the feet of the Lakeview number ten, Ravi Mistry, and the striker steered it low into the corner of the net.

'Tough luck,' said Chris Vaughan, the captain, to his dejected goalie. 'Not your fault.'

'I know that. Where was the defence?' he moaned. 'Both those kids got free shots.'

Chris shrugged, knowing Nidesh was right, and booted the ball away upfield to relieve his frustration. 'C'mon, men, tighten up,' he urged, clapping his hands. 'We can't let them do that again.'

'Well played, Blues,' called out Miss Jackson as the teams lined up for the restart. 'You deserved that.'

Harry gazed at the Lakeview P.E. teacher. Joe had told him all about Jacko, as he called her, but this was the first time that Harry had seen her. 'Wish she was at the Comp instead of old Yardley,' he grunted.

Harry had not got off to the best of starts with Mr Yardley. He'd brought himself to the teacher's attention at the first soccer trial by accidentally hitting him on the back of the head with the ball. Relations between them had gone downhill ever since.

The rest of this game was rather like that for Lakeview. The Great Danton pitch was on a slope and although the visitors were now kicking down, they could not turn that supposed advantage into further goals. The ball tended to keep running away from them out of play.

With the home team playing more controlled football up the slope, the equalizer looked increasingly likely. And with just five minutes left on the referee's watch, it finally came. The shot was hit more in hope than expectation from outside the penalty area, but it took a slight deflection off a defender's outstretched foot – Joe's. The ball bounced awkwardly in front of Elvis's dive, squirmed through his grasp and just had enough strength to bobble over the line.

Adam Quinn was quick to claim the credit. 'My goal,' he cried as his teammates mobbed him.

'Nice one, Q,' laughed the captain. 'Didn't think you'd let us put that down to an own goal.'

Joe was busy insisting the same thing after the match. 'My touch didn't make any difference. It would've gone in anyway,' he said in the car on the way home.

Harry smirked. 'I don't think your keeper would agree.'

'The shot was too good for Elvis,' Joe argued. 'It was just like one of my skimmers on the lake – at least a tenner!'

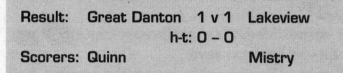

Result: Great Danton   1 v 1   Lakeview
                       h-t: 0 – 0
Scorers: Quinn   Mistry

MEDVILLE v NEEDHAM COLLEGE

Saturday 11 October
k.o. 10 a.m.
Referee: Mr S. Yardley

. . . edited highlights for anyone, like Harry, who missed the game . . .

 **FIRST HALF**

2 mins: first scoring chance of cup-tie squandered by College as Baker shoots wide of open goal

5 mins: Medville's goalkeeper-captain Burns pulls off brilliant save

7 mins: Burns again in action, turning ball round post for another corner – angry at his team's poor start to the match

11 mins: College keeper at last has to make a save – tips Yorke's header over crossbar

12 mins: Bridges scores for Medville after corner results in goalmouth scramble, poking ball over line

17 mins: College under increasing pressure as Medville find rhythm – D.J. Williams kept busy in goal

20 mins: College woodwork rattled twice in same attack – Bridges hits post then Montgomery scoops rebound onto crossbar

25 mins: goal number two for Medville – Joyner nets after good work by full-back Twigg, overlapping up right wing

28 mins: timely reminder for home team just before interval that match isn't yet won – College captain Parmar fires into side netting with Burns beaten

half-time: Medville 2 v 0 Needham College

 ## SECOND HALF

1 min: College caught cold by swift attack from kick-off – rescued by reflexes of Williams, saving from Bridges at point-blank range

3 mins: Medville penalty appeals turned down after Bridges claims a trip

7 mins: Parmar scores but 'goal' disallowed for offside – furious protests from College supporters on touchline

10 mins: College win direct free-kick for handball just outside area and Wright lashes it over defensive wall into net – score 2–1 – Burns speechless with rage

16 mins: Medville force third successive corner in good spell of pressure

18 mins: Medville substitute, Maan, almost restores two-goal lead with his first touch, screwing ball just wide of upright

21 mins: College centre-back Haynes heads shot off line

22 mins: Burns makes save of the game to

28

prevent equalizer after breakaway College raid, diving full-length to catch Wright's fierce volley

27 mins: Montgomery clinches victory for Medville, slipping Maan's pass under Williams

30 mins: Medville well on top – both Bridges and Joyner go close to adding a fourth goal before final whistle

Result:	Medville	3 v 1	Needham College
	h-t:	2 – 0	
Scorers:	Bridges		Wright
	Joyner		
	Montgomery		

HARD TIMES

. . scene: Medville Comprehensive on Monday morning, where Harry is made to feel an outsider in his own form room . . .

'Where were *you* on Saturday?'

'What do you mean?'

'You know what I mean all right – traitor!'

Harry was squashed up in a corner of the room, confronted by a leering group of footballers. The school team captain, Ryan Burns, continued his inquisition, jabbing a finger into Harry's chest as he spoke.

'You went to watch the other lot play, didn't you?'

Harry saw there was no point in trying to deny the accusation. 'Well, what if I did? What's it to you?'

'Plenty! We don't like anybody here being all pally with the enemy.'

'My cousin plays for Lakeview.'

'I couldn't care less. You should've been here to support us, not them.'

'Unless you were really on a *spying* mission, of course,' sneered another player.

'Fat chance of that, Monty. Can you imagine this wally as the new James Bond?' Ryan cackled. 'Harry Glenn – secret agent – 003$\frac{1}{2}$!'

'C'mon, then, Harry, spill the beans,' said Adam Bridges, smirking. 'What are those other two teams like? Tell us all their weaknesses.'

Harry remained silent. Even if he'd had anything to report, which he didn't, they were clearly in no mood for listening.

Ryan shoved a desk hard against Harry's legs, trapping him against the wall. 'Well, I'll tell you something, shall I, Glenn?' he snarled. 'You're rubbish! You hear that? A waste of space. You're not fit to be in our squad.'

'Yeah, let's hope when Yardley finds out you deserted the Comp, he'll kick you out,' Monty sniggered. 'Serves you right if he did.'

'C'mon, leave him now, he's not worth it,' said Paramjit, the only one of the footballers who had gone to the same primary school as Harry.

Ryan gave the desk another firm shove. 'Yeah, come on, guys. Pity you, Pram-Man, having to put up with that wimp last year too.'

The others slouched away with Ryan, leaving Harry and Paramjit together briefly. Harry slipped him a quick smile of thanks.

'Sorry I had to say that about you, Harry. Seemed the only way to get them off your back.'

'It wasn't my back I was worried about,' he replied, rubbing his sore thighs.

'I'd keep a low profile for a bit, if I were you.'

Harry nodded. 'Good idea. Think I'll skip the practice this week. They never pass to me, anyway – nobody will miss me.'

. . . try and put yourself in Harry's shoes – how would you feel in his situation at the moment? . . .

PASS AND MOVE

. . . if you can resist the stunning view over Lake Medd, watch Miss Jackson put her squad through their paces in an after-school training session . . .

'That's good, boys, keep it going,' the Lakeview coach called out. 'Control, pass and run . . . head up, Ravi . . . sharper, Joe, only two touches needed . . . keep that ball moving . . . sprint, Michael, don't be lazy . . .'

Miss Jackson was quick to pounce on anybody who wasn't trying their hardest. Her shrill voice seemed to echo out over the lake and back again, broadcasting their name and their sins to the world.

'Jacko's a slave-driver,' panted Elvis during a brief respite while the teacher rearranged some cones. 'I'm half dead.'

'About time you did some running and took a bit of that weight off,' chuckled Ben, the captain. 'Jacko says goalies need to be just as fit as us outfield players.'

'Don't see why,' he grumbled.

'Because the fitter you are, the better, that's why. You've often got to come dashing out of your goal for the ball. No good being a tortoise.'

'Yeah, well,' he shrugged, 'you know the old fable about the hare and the tortoise . . .'

'Yes, but they weren't playing soccer, were they?' Ben replied, squashing that excuse from his pal.

'Can't complain, really,' said Joe. 'I mean, Jacko's super-fit herself. She has to do all this kind of training as well for her own team, y'know.'

'Come on, you lads, no time to sit around gossiping,' Miss Jackson said, smiling. 'We need to do some work on those passing skills of yours. They're not good enough yet, judging by the last couple of games.'

'Oh, miss, we did win the other day,' whined Matthew Tudor, known to all his mates as Henry after a history project on the Tudors at primary school. He was referring to their midweek league match when he and Ravi shared the goals in a 2–0 victory.

'Yes, but we were outpassed for most of that game,' she pointed out. 'We only won because they couldn't shoot straight.'

'Not to mention my saves of course,' Elvis put in, then added sadly, 'Not that anybody has mentioned them yet, I've noticed.'

'OK, Michael,' laughed the teacher, resisting the temptation to use his nickname. 'You did play very well. Consider them mentioned.'

The goalkeeper beamed at the praise, forgiving Miss Jackson instantly for all the torture she had been inflicting upon them.

'Good, now that Michael's happy, let's get on,' she said. 'It's important we don't waste possession. Good teams don't give the ball away carelessly. They make it hard for the opposition to get it back again.'

As they practised, Miss Jackson demonstrated how various passes should be made, using different parts of her feet to hit short and long balls along the ground or in the air. The players were so absorbed in their attempts to copy her technique that there were none of the usual requests for a game before the coach herself decided it was time.

'Well done, not bad at all for a bunch of beginners,' she teased. 'I'll be awarding extra brownie points now for good passes in the four-a-sides.'

Only Ravi seemed somewhat out of sorts in the hectic games that followed. He was Lakeview's leading scorer so far this season, but his usual energy and spark were missing.

'What's the matter, Ravi?' Miss Jackson asked as they were all walking back into school to change and go home. 'Is something bothering you?'

'Sorry, miss,' he said, almost filling up with tears. 'It's just that I had some bad news today.'

'Oh dear – do you want to talk about it?'

'Dad's got a new job, like, and it means us moving house,' he blurted out. 'I'll be leaving here soon.'

He broke into a run towards the school and the teacher was left rooted to the spot, open-mouthed. She was wondering just *how* soon that would be.

. . . Even Ravi didn't know whether he'd still be at Lakeview when they played their next Cup match – the key local Derby clash with their big rivals at Medville Comprehensive . . .

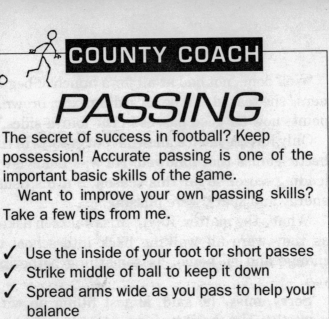

COUNTY COACH

PASSING

The secret of success in football? Keep possession! Accurate passing is one of the important basic skills of the game.

Want to improve your own passing skills? Take a few tips from me.

- ✓ Use the inside of your foot for short passes
- ✓ Strike middle of ball to keep it down
- ✓ Spread arms wide as you pass to help your balance
- ✓ Place non-kicking foot alongside ball, pointing towards target
- ✓ Control the pace (weight) of the pass, depending on distance
- ✓ Practise hard to improve passing with your weaker foot too
- ✓ Longer passes often have to be lofted or chipped over opponents
- ✓ Lean back slightly and strike low part of ball with your instep
- ✓ Chip a pass by stabbing at bottom of ball with toes
- ✓ Practise passing with the outside of the foot too
- ✓ Keep practising

WHAT A PASS!

TRICK OR TREAT

. . . it's Friday night and we're down at lake level once more, but beware – it's also Halloween! . . .

'Guessed I might find you here, Harry,' Joe greeted him. 'Called round at your house and your dad said you'd already gone out.'

There were two figures sitting on the wall by the lakeside in the gloom. Joe didn't recognize the other boy next to his cousin.

'This is Pram-Man,' said Harry. 'He's a mate from the Comp. Sorry, correction – he's my *only* mate at the Comp.'

'Hi, I'm Joe . . .'

'Yeah, I know who you are,' Paramjit grinned, cutting him short. 'I'm playing against you in the Cup tomorrow – and so's Harry.'

'Hey, that's great . . .' Joe began, then faltered as he saw Harry's downcast face. '. . . Isn't it? I thought you wanted to be in the team.'

'I'm only one of the subs.'

'Well, that's OK. You might get to come on.'

'That's what I keep telling him,' said Paramjit. 'I've been sub a few times, but I've got a place in the side now Yardley's made changes after our last league game. He nearly went berserk when we lost!'

'Heard about that,' Joe smirked. 'Last-minute goal, wasn't it?'

'Yeah – miles offside. We all stopped playing, waiting for the whistle.'

Harry butted in. 'Shows how desperate old Yardley must be, picking me. He doesn't even know my name properly. He always calls me Glenn.'

Joe shrugged. 'We've got a science teacher who only uses our surnames.'

'It's not that,' Harry sighed. 'He seems to think Glenn's my first name.'

'You should put him right.'

'Can't be bothered. Most of the other kids have started calling me Glenn now.'

'There are worse nicknames to have than your own surname.'

'Yeah, like mine,' muttered Paramjit.

'The best way to get them to stop bugging you, I reckon, is to play a stormer. Y'know, score the winning goal or something,' said Joe, then checked himself. 'Only not against us, OK? You can play the big hero next week instead.'

'Come off it!' Harry snorted. 'That sort of thing only happens in stories. Knowing my luck, I'm more likely to go and put through my own goal. They'd probably lynch me then.'

'Who are these guys, anyway? I can give them a good whack in the match if you point them out to me before kick-off.'

'I can do that now,' Harry said with a groan. 'They're heading this way.'

'Well, well, look who it isn't!' cackled Monty. 'It's little Glenn, our new supersub.'

'Surprised to see you here, Pram-Man,' said Ryan. 'Thought you had more sense than to knock around with losers like him still.'

'Leave off him, will you,' said Paramjit. 'Harry's OK when you get to know him.'

'Don't know any Harry,' sneered Adam. 'Unless it's this other kid.'

Joe stepped forward, his fists clenching. 'You'll find out who I am soon enough in the morning.'

Ryan turned to his mates and sniggered. 'Looks like we've found cousin Joe, guys.'

Harry spoke up before Joe could take any rash action. 'What are you three doing here, anyway?'

'It's Halloween, Glenn, don't you even know that?' scoffed Ryan. 'Good night for getting away with things.'

'Yeah, trick or treat, Glenn?' said Monty menacingly. 'Take your pick.'

Paramjit looked puzzled. 'Trick or treat?'

'You stay out of this, Pram-Man,' said Adam. 'You won't understand our old customs. Got nothing to do with your lot.'

'What do you mean, my lot?' he said, bristling with indignation. 'I was born in this country, just like you. I understood that trick or treat was only done by little kids in fancy dress.'

'You mean they always look like this?' Joe put in. 'I thought they were wearing ugly goblin masks!'

It was only with difficulty that Ryan's gang ignored the insult. They weren't quite sure of Paramjit's reaction if they got involved in a brawl. He was a big lad. The captain decided to put him to the test.

'Whose side are you on here, Pram-Man?' he asked.

'No need to take sides,' came back the careful answer. 'You know where my loyalties will lie tomorrow.'

'This is tonight. Don't say you haven't had your chance.'

'So trick or treat, Glenn?' Monty repeated.

'Got nothing I want to give you.'

'Right, trick it is, then,' said Adam. 'What's it gonna be?'

Ryan smirked. 'We could dunk him in the lake . . .'

'I'd like to see you try,' muttered Joe.

'Or even bring the lake here – OK, let 'em have it!'

Before Paramjit and the cousins could take evasive action, the gang had whipped washing-up liquid bottles from their coat pockets and squirted them with water. The tricksters' quickness on the draw was only matched by their speed off the mark. By the time their victims had recovered from their surprise, they were already disappearing round a corner into the town. Any chase would have been in vain.

'Ugh!' Joe exclaimed in disgust as he saw the stain down the front of his coat. 'It wasn't just water in them bottles. They've put a blue dye in it – ink or something. Mum'll kill me.'

'Mine won't,' said Harry. 'She won't even see it.'

Joe laughed. 'You'll be lucky. If I know my aunt, she'll spot it as soon as you try and sneak back in. She doesn't miss a thing.'

'She'll miss this. She's not there.'

'How d'yer mean?'

'Mum and Dad had a big row last night and she walked out, slamming the door.'

Joe could hardly believe it. 'Where's she gone?'

'Gran's, I think, I'm not sure. Dad's not said much.'

'What were they arguing about?'

Harry sighed. 'Me, probably. I've told them I want to leave the Comp and they can't agree what to do. Dad wants me to stay and try to tough it out. Says I've got to learn to stick up for myself.'

The cousins lapsed into an embarrassed silence, uncertain what to say next, and it was Paramjit who finally gave a little cough and spoke. 'Um . . . best if we all went home and got cleaned up, I suppose.'

Joe nodded. 'Make sure you wash that blue off your face,' he replied, forcing a grin. 'That's our colours. You don't want that lot thinking you've become a Lakeview supporter now!'

The cousins set off in the same direction for a while before they had to go their separate ways.

'They're not going to be allowed to get away with this,' said Joe with determination. 'I'll pay them back somehow . . .'

   'Not worth the hassle,' Harry muttered. 'Right now, Ryan and his gang are the least of my problems.'

LAKEVIEW v MEDVILLE

Saturday 1 November
k.o. 10 a.m.
Referee: Miss R. Jackson

... all set for the local Derby? Ravi will be making his final appearance for Lakeview, but there's somebody else missing – where's Harry? ...

Mr Yardley was fuming as he stalked out of the changing rooms. 'Typical! You give the boy a chance and he can't even be bothered to turn up.'

Miss Jackson was sitting on a low bench outside, tying up her boots. 'What's the matter?' she asked, glancing up.

'We've been let down by one of our subs,' said the Comp's P.E. teacher. 'He'd better have some very good excuse or he's had it now. I won't pick him again.'

Except for Paramjit, the Comp players didn't think that Harry's no-show was any great loss. 'He's got a few problems at home,' his friend said. 'I expect that's why he's not here.'

'Huh! Bet it's 'cos he daren't face us after last night,' scoffed Ryan. 'Glad to see you've got more bottle, Pram-Man.'

'You were the ones with bottles,' he replied sourly.

Harry's absence had not gone unnoticed by his cousin of course. Joe was still looking out for him as he warmed up, hoping to see his late, breathless arrival, but then he had to put Harry out of his mind for a while. Jacko had blown the whistle for the kick-off.

The Halloween encounter by the lake had given this game an even keener edge, as far as Joe was concerned. He was after revenge. Nothing would give him greater pleasure than putting the ball past the Comp captain in goal.

His first clash, however, was with Monty. They were in direct opposition on the pitch, Joe playing right wing-back for the Blues and Monty left-side midfield for the Reds. Neither of them backed off from their early, bone-jarring challenge for a 50–50 ball, and they thundered into one another like a pair of stags locking antlers in a battle for dominance.

Miss Jackson gave a free-kick to the visitors. 'You both went in too hard,' she said to them sternly. 'Calm down and shake hands, boys.'

There was a moment's reluctance to do as instructed, followed by the briefest of palm contact, as if the other had some contagious disease.

'Round one to me,' smirked Monty as he trotted away, but Joe spotted a slight hint of a limp.

'Not so sure about that,' he murmured.

The free-kick was overhit, floating into Elvis's hands in the Lakeview goal, and he immediately threw the ball out to his left wing-back to start a counter-attack. The move looked promising. Dan linked up with the captain in midfield and then Ben steered the ball wide to Ravi with the outside of his foot, disguising the pass well.

'Nice one, Ben,' hissed the referee as she ran by, pleased that all their recent passing practice might be paying dividends.

Then Ravi went and spoiled it. He tried to do too much on the ball, dribbling along the touchline, and finally lost possession. Miss Jackson felt like calling something out but just managed to check herself. Her criticism would have to wait till half-time.

The interval eventually arrived with the scoreline still blank. The two well-matched teams were tending to cancel each other out. Defences were on top and neither keeper had been unduly troubled, apart from when Ryan had to scramble across his goal to turn aside a dipping effort from Dan.

'Let's see you pushing forward more often, Joe,' Miss Jackson told him as the players gathered around her. 'You're having too much of a running battle with that number six of theirs. Make him have to mark you a bit more in their own half of the pitch.'

'He's already left one or two marks on me,' he said, showing her a graze above his knee where Monty had caught him with a high tackle.

'Yes, I know, I warned him for that. But don't try and retaliate or you'll be in trouble with me. Stick to playing football, right?'

Joe nodded. 'OK, miss, I'll make him regret it another way.'

'Good, you do that. I expect my wing-backs to get a few goals and don't think I haven't noticed your name isn't on the scoresheet yet.'

'How many goals have you got this season, miss?' he asked cheekily.

'Two more than you,' she said with a grin.

SECOND HALF

. . . the deadlock is immediately broken by an unexpected flurry of goals, but none of them scored by Joe . . .

★ **Scoreflash**: *Lakeview 0–1 Medville*

Adam Bridges shoots the visitors ahead in their first attack, drilling the ball into the net after a slick move carves open the Lakeview defence . . .

★ **Scoreflash**: *Lakeview 1–1 Medville*

A rare lapse of concentration in the Comp's defence allows Ravi Mistry to give his team-mates a farewell present, stroking the ball home after Matthew Tudor bursts past two casual tackles . . .

★ **Scoreflash**: *Lakeview 1–2 Medville*

Within a minute, Paramjit Maan's lofted pass sends Robin Yorke away on a clear run at goal, the winger restoring the Comp's lead by slipping the ball through the advancing keeper's legs . . .

When the dust settled after such an explosive start, the Lakeview players were staring at an embarrassing early exit from the County Cup. A second win for the Comp would put them out of reach at the top of the group table.

Without Elvis's reflexes – and a generous measure of luck when Adam's header bounced off the crossbar – Lakeview's task might already have been hopeless. In a frantic goalmouth scramble, the keeper made an instinctive block, throwing out an arm to deflect the ball around the post.

Elvis was suddenly inspired. He leapt high to catch the corner cleanly, landed on his toes and hurled the ball out wide, almost in one movement. The quick clearance caught the attacking side off guard and nobody was able to make a challenge on Joe as he strode over the halfway line with the ball. He looked round for someone to pass to, but all he could see were chasing red shirts – so he just carried on running deeper into enemy territory.

He was aware of the goalkeeper coming out to meet him and after a long run almost the length of the field, his tired legs didn't have the spring in them to evade Ryan's desperate lunge. Joe's last touch on the ball pushed it wide of the goalie's grasp and then his world was turned upside-down. The force of hitting the ground knocked all the remaining breath out of his body.

'Penalty!' cried the home supporters as Ryan jumped angrily to his feet.

'Never touched him, ref – he dived,' he shouted. 'Anyway, it was outside the area.'

Neither excuse worked. Miss Jackson was already pointing to the spot. Only her level of fitness had allowed her to be up with play and see that the foul had actually been committed inside the penalty area, whatever the goalkeeper and the linesman might be claiming.

Miss Jackson didn't expect an unbiased view from the linesman, but as Mr Yardley was still waving his flag furiously, she went over to speak to him. 'Do you agree that it was a foul?' she asked.

'Well, yes,' he said, somewhat reluctantly. 'My goalie did clatter into him – but it wasn't in the box, I'm sure.'

'Who was closer to the action? Me or you?'

Mr Yardley also had to admit that the speed of the breakaway had left him out of position. 'Well, you were, I suppose . . .'

'Good, I'm glad we agree on those two things – because I say it happened inside the area, and that's why my decision is a penalty.'

Her manner made it clear there was no room

for argument. As she walked away, she thought she heard some mutterings about female referees, but chose to turn a deaf ear.

'You take it, Ben,' she said to the captain.

Ben already had the ball in his hand. He knew that it was his responsibility. He placed the ball carefully on the penalty spot and waited for the referee's signal, ignoring Ryan's attempts to distract him.

The delay had given Joe a chance to recover and he stood on the edge of the area with the other players to watch the penalty drama. The whistle blew, Ben ran forward and hit the ball low to Ryan's left. The kick was good – but the diving save was even better, knocking the ball out to one side. Joe was out of his blocks like an Olympic sprinter and reached the spinning, rolling ball an instant before Monty crunched into him from behind.

If the ball hadn't zipped into the net, Miss Jackson would have given another penalty, but the goal was punishment enough. Joe was buried under an avalanche of celebrating teammates, trapping Monty in the crush of bodies on the ground, which didn't exactly improve his temper. When Joe was allowed to struggle to his feet, he caught Monty's eye and then glanced at Ryan in triumph. He didn't need to say anything. The goal he'd just scored had said it all.

By comparison with such controversy, the rest of the match was surprisingly uneventful, with both sides having to be content in the end with a point apiece from the 2–2 draw. The teachers shook hands formally but relations were strained. Miss Jackson was glad to stay out of what she imagined would be a hostile atmosphere in the boys' changing room.

The first person to emerge was Joe – only because he hadn't bothered to change out of his football kit.

'Didn't want to hang about in there,' he said, grinning at his teacher. 'I'll have a bath at home.'

'Can't say I blame you,' Miss Jackson smiled.

'Now it's only one more than me, miss.'

'What is?' she asked, puzzled, not quite picking up his meaning.

'Your goal tally,' he laughed and trailed away, weary but happy.

Result:	Lakeview 2 v 2	Medville
	h-t: 0–0	
Scorers:	Mistry	Bridges
	Vernon	Yorke

. . . why not work out the group table yourself at this stage to see how all the teams stand? It's three points for a win and one for a draw – but remember that Great Danton and the College both have a game in hand now . . .

SEARCH PARTIES

. . . sadly, all thoughts of football are soon banished from Joe's mind – tune in to the Saturday night news on Radio Medland to find out what's happened . . .

'Fears are growing for the safety of the young boy who was reported missing earlier today in Medville. Eleven-year-old Harry Glenn left home this morning to play in a school football match but failed to arrive. A sports bag containing his soccer kit was later seen beside Lake Medd by his cousin . . .

'. . . A police spokesman said that no clues had yet been found as to the boy's whereabouts. Searches will resume at first light, when police frogmen and members of the Medville Diving Club will also be called in to help . . .'

Joe switched off the bedside radio and slumped back on to his pillow, exhausted after hunting for his cousin most of the day. Groups of local people, friends, family and neighbours had all joined the police in scouring the town and surrounding countryside for the boy.

'Oh, Harry,' he murmured. 'What have you gone and done? Where are you?'

Those questions remained unanswered the following day. The teams of divers spent hours exploring the dark, choppy waters of Lake Medd without success. Joe had watched their efforts anxiously from the shore, desperately hoping they wouldn't actually find anything – or anybody.

'Stephen . . .'
  'Here.'
  'Mark . . .'
  'Here.'
  'Harry . . .'
There was a deathly hush in Harry's form room as his name was unexpectedly called out on Monday morning. The teacher looked up from the register and turned bright red. 'Oh, goodness, I . . . I'm sorry,' he stumbled, flustered. 'I didn't mean to say his name. It's just habit . . . I'm sorry, everyone.'

There were a few stifled sobs around the room, while the footballers caught each other's eyes, uncertain how to react. Ryan spoke out. 'It's all right, Mr Blake, I bet Harry will turn up OK sometime. He's probably just run off for some reason.'

The school team captain didn't like to dwell on the thought that he might be partly responsible for Harry's disappearance. Like Adam and Monty, he was already regretting the things he'd been saying – and doing – to him.

The teacher was trying to recover his composure. 'Well, let's all hope you're right, Ryan,' Mr Blake said. 'We shall be going into the hall this morning for a special assembly to pray for Harry's safe return.'

Harry's name was also mentioned in assembly at Lakeview High School, but Joe was not there to hear the headteacher's warnings to his pupils about not speaking to any strangers. Joe was in no frame of mind to attend school. He had been down at the lakeside since dawn, standing in the rain to watch the divers prepare to resume their searches.

A terrible feeling of helplessness overcame him and he wandered away. He needed to be alone, with time and space to think. Joe set off along one of the tracks that skirted the edge of the lake, a route that he and Harry often used when they went fishing together. He pulled back the hood of his coat and let the wind ruffle his long hair and the drizzle run down his face. He was already too wet to care.

Joe rounded the corner of the lake and continued up the western shoreline, a path well-trampled over the weekend by the various search parties. 'I'll just go as far as the old boathouse, then turn back,' he decided. 'Don't want Mum and Dad raising the alarm for me as well.'

When he reached the ramshackle boathouse, he scrambled down to where the water washed up against its splintered timbers and peered inside – just in case. It was empty, as always, except for a few pieces of rusting equipment and a half-submerged wreck of a rowing boat.

Joe scooped up a handful of loose stones from the shore, selected the flatter ones and booted the rest up in the air. His first effort managed only a couple of skips before sinking without trace, but the second survived a little longer.

'Not bad – about a fiver that, I reckon.'

Joe whirled round at the sound of the voice. He was too flabbergasted to speak for a moment – and then made up for it. 'And where the hell have you been?' he demanded, before bombarding his cousin with a barrage of questions.

Harry shrugged them off. 'Just decided to run away,' he said.

'Where to?'

'Didn't matter about the *to*. It was the *from* that seemed more important at the time.'

'But people have been looking all over for you.'

'Yeah, seen them. I had to keep hiding. I didn't know anyone cared.'

'The whole town cares, you idiot,' Joe stormed in his rage of relief. 'The whole county! They've even had your picture on television.'

Harry looked amazed. 'Which one?'

'*Which one?*' Joe repeated. 'Is that all you can say? Right this minute, divers are fishing around for you at the bottom of the lake. Your parents are going mad with worry.'

'Are they back together?'

'Course they are. Is that why you did a runner? 'Cos of their row?'

'Sort of, I guess. Things just got on top of me.

I couldn't face turning up at the match. What was the score, by the way?'

'Never mind about that. Let's just get you back home. You must have been freezing out here at night.'

He slung an arm around his cousin and made sure Harry couldn't resist going with him.

'I'm gonna be in even more trouble now, aren't I, for wasting people's time,' Harry whimpered.

'I shouldn't worry about that,' Joe reassured him. 'Reckon they'll just be so pleased to see you again. You must be starving.'

Harry pulled a hand from his coat pocket and offered Joe a piece of chocolate. 'That's my last bit. You can have it, if you want.'

'No thanks, it's all squashed,' he grinned. 'Hey! Why don't you come up to my school tonight? There'll be loads of food there to stuff down your throat. We've got a big bonfire on the playing field for a joint celebration of Bonfire Night and Diwali.'

'Doubt if Mum and Dad will let me go after what I've done.'

'Yes, they will. I'll tell them it'll give you a chance to meet some of your future teammates,' Joe babbled on. 'Well, apart from Ravi, that is. He's leaving this week . . .'

Harry interrupted him. 'My future team-mates? What do you mean?'

'Oops, me and my big mouth!' gulped Joe. 'Soz, it's just that I heard my uncle say you could go to Lakeview if you really hated the Comp so much.'

Harry didn't know whether to laugh or cry. His emotions were still all mixed up. 'What if your crowd start making fun of me as well?' he croaked.

'Course they won't. They're not like that. Anyway, you're a star now – you're famous! They'll all be dead glad to see you.'

'Well, OK, if I can,' Harry said, forcing a smile. 'So long as you tell me all about what happened in the Cup . . .'

. . . wonder what kind of reception awaits Harry when he shows up again with Joe – how do you think his parents and other people will react? . . .

AT THE COLLEGE

. . . while all this drama is taking place in Medville, over at Pedley the College squad have been quietly preparing for the visit of Great Danton . . .

'**R**ight, we're going to work on some set-piece routines today, lads,' said Mr O'Donald, the College teacher. 'Corners and free-kicks around the box.'

The players liked the sound of that. They had already scored half a dozen goals this season from dead-ball situations, including Tom Wright's superb effort against the Comp. Their leading striker wasn't slow to remind his team-mates of that goal now.

'That area team keeper of theirs never smelt it,' he boasted. 'The ball flew right into the top corner.'

'Yeah, yeah, we saw it,' laughed Paul, the left-winger. 'You're not the only one who's scored from a direct free-kick, you know. What about my beauty against Lakeview in the league?'

'That took a deflection. Mine didn't need any help.'

'It doesn't matter how they go in,' said Jayesh, the captain. 'Let's just hope we get the chance to convert one or two more on Saturday.'

Tom grinned. 'Should do – O'Donald's the ref!'

The teacher split the footballers into groups to practise, but he kept his dead-ball specialists together and supervised them closely. Three of them were strikers, Jayesh, Tom and Paul, plus right-back Mark Jewell.

'It's up to the captain who takes a free-kick in a match,' Mr O'Donald told them. 'It might depend on which side of the goal the kick's from – whether it favours a left- or right-footed strike – or how far out it is.'

There was no keeper to beat today. The teacher's instruction was simply to try and make sure they hit the target. Tom and Mark tended to rely on sheer power, but Paul and the captain often managed to put quite a swerve on the ball too. The reward for accuracy was that the net saved the shooter from having to fetch the ball.

Paul's left-footed, curling dipper into the bottom corner was judged the best effort, but Jayesh had to make the fewest treks behind the goal. He put four of his five attempts into the net.

The session ended with the whole squad practising corners. Some acted as defenders while the others tried to escape their marking. Callum was dominant in the air, as always, either in defence or attack. The tall centre-back brought a brilliant save out of the keeper from one of Paul's in-swinging corners. D.J. flung himself high to his left to touch the powerful header over the crossbar.

'Magic, D.J.!' cried Tom. 'Hope you're in that kind of form on Saturday.'

They were all going to need to be on top form. Great Danton had already beaten them 3–2 in a league match and the College were eager for revenge.

'It'll be different now we're at home,' said Callum confidently. 'They won't have their sloping pitch to help them. We're gonna stuff 'em!'

'Sure hope so,' said Mark. ''Cos if we lose again, we'll be out of the Cup.'

. . . how successful are your team's set-piece tactics? See what the County Coach has to say on the subject . . .

SET-PIECE TACTICS –
ATTACKING

Football is a team game. Corners and free-kicks need good teamwork to be effective. This takes time and practice on the training ground so that everybody knows what to do and where they should be, Want to improve your team's dead-ball tactics? Take a few tips from me.

✓ Choose left- and right-footed kickers who can strike a dead ball cleanly
✓ Make them practise – and practise – their skills
✓ Corners – vary tactics, short & long, in-swingers & out-swingers
✓ Have someone in front of near post to flick ball on across goal
✓ Practise dodging skills to lose markers in crowded penalty areas
✓ Free-kicks – practise curling/swerving ball over or round defensive wall
✓ Try to disguise who will shoot, making dummy runs off the ball
✓ Copy clever moves seen on television matches
✓ Keep practising

WHAT A SHOT!!

NEEDHAM COLLEGE v GREAT DANTON

Saturday 8 November
k.o. 9.30 a.m.
Referee: Mr F. O'Donald

. . . sorry, it was an early kick-off and you've missed the first-half action – the College are about to restart the game, trailing 1–0 and hoping for better luck in the second period . . .

'C'mon, team, get stuck in,' yelled the College goalkeeper, standing on the edge of his penalty area as Jayesh and Tom kicked off.

David 'D.J.' Williams had done his best to keep his team in the game before the interval. He'd made two splendid saves, but a long-range shot from Great Danton's right-back had proved unstoppable. The same opponent was soon threatening a repeat performance and D.J. had to backtrack quickly to protect his goal.

'Let's have another from you, Woody,' cried a spectator as the full-back charged upfield with the ball. 'Have a crack.'

Brian Woods certainly had that in mind, but

this time his run was halted by the keeper's namesake, David 'Dazza' Williams. Dazza robbed him of the ball with a firm tackle and lofted it back into the Danton half, leaving Woody out of position. College winger Paul Allen was in the clear until a covering defender raced across and tripped him up just outside the penalty area.

'Direct free-kick – brill! Just what we've been practising,' grinned Tom. 'Who's taking this one, Jay?'

'I am,' replied the captain, placing the ball on the ground. 'It's in the perfect position for one of my right-footed curlers.'

Tom didn't argue. 'I'll do a dummy over the ball first, and then you follow up behind me, OK?'

Jayesh nodded. 'OK, but make sure you get out of the way.'

Mr O'Donald insisted that the red-striped defensive wall went another two paces further away from the ball and then blew his whistle. Tom ran in, looking just as if he was going to strike the ball – and he did. He hit it straight and true but the wall did its job. The ball crashed into a defender's legs and bounced harmlessly away.

Jayesh was furious. 'I said I was taking it.'

'Soz, Jay, just forgot,' Tom replied, giving a sly shrug of the shoulders. 'Got a bit carried away there.'

'You didn't forget at all. You were just being greedy.'

'On with the game,' snapped the referee as he jogged past. 'Sort it out later.'

The College had to withstand five minutes of heavy pressure as Great Danton strove for a match-winning second goal. Wingers Kyle and Paul worked hard to support their own full-backs and Jayesh dropped deeper to bolster the midfield, leaving only Tom upfield. Their goal enjoyed a charmed life. The crossbar was rattled by a header from the Danton number nine, Adam Quinn, and two efforts from his strike-partner were cleared off the line.

'Bad luck, Ishy,' said Q as the ball was scrambled away again. 'Deserved a goal.'

'Just can't seem to score in the County Cup,' moaned Sam Isherwood. 'I've got four in the league.'

Q grinned. 'Still not as many as me.'

Great Danton were to rue those missed chances. The College survived and hit the visitors on the break, catching them over-committed to the attack. A swift inter-passing move between Mark and Kyle along the right touchline resulted in a low cross that Jayesh steered past the keeper into the net for a surprise equalizer.

Mr O'Donald took the opportunity to make a substitution, bringing on Philip Cork – known to his mates as Champagne – for the last quarter of an hour. Tom paid the price for his behaviour over the free-kick and was stunned to find himself replaced. He snatched his tracksuit top from his watching mother and leant against the fence, sulking.

'Hope we go and lose now,' he muttered under his breath.

Tom didn't get his wish. The equalizing goal changed the course of the game. The College players grew in confidence and the ball now spent most of its time in their opponents' half. Great Danton could only try desperately to hold on for a draw to keep alive their own hopes of qualification.

The decisive moment came from another free-kick when Jayesh was brought down by a wild tackle. The kick was too far out for one of his own curlers to be effective. It was more Tom's sort of range, but he was off the pitch now. The captain summoned Mark instead.

'Have a go, Mark. Really let rip. If anybody gets in the way, make them regret it.'

Mark's thunderbolt flashed wide of the wall but Nidesh in goal had it well covered. All he could do, though, was parry the ball. It was too hot to handle. Before Nidesh could dive to smother the rebound, Champagne darted forward and poked the ball over the line.

'Champagne Cork pops up for the winner!' laughed Paul as the scorer was hauled back to the centre-circle by his celebrating teammates.

It would have made a good newspaper headline – and proved an equally good forecast of the final result.

A sheet of paper mysteriously appeared on the College's sports noticeboard on Monday morning. Ratings out of ten had been given to each of the players for their performances in the Cup game.

```
Man of the (1/4) Match — Champagne Cork
D.J. Williams — 8,
Jewell — 8,
Hope — 6,
Haynes — 8,
Dazza Williams — 7,
Simmons — 6
(sub: Owen — 6),
Zaturowski — 7,
Baker — 7,
Parmar (capt) — 9,
Wright — 4
(sub: Cork — 10),
Allen — 8.
```

Nobody owned up to doing it, but the general suspicion fell upon the grinning Champagne. Tom Wright certainly didn't find the spoof form guide very funny. He tore it off the board and ripped the paper up into little pieces.

CUP STATS

Latest match

Result: Needham College 2 v 1 Great Danton
h-t: 0 – 1

Scorers: Parmar   Woods
Cork

GROUP TABLE

	P	W	D	L	Goals F	A	(GD)	Pts
Medville	2	1	1	0	5	3	(+2)	4
Needham College	2	1	0	1	3	4	(−1)	3
Lakeview	2	0	2	0	3	3	(0)	2
Great Danton	2	0	1	1	2	3	(−1)	1

Analysis

The race for the East Quarter Championship remains wide open. Any of the four schools could still finish top of the group table and qualify for the semi-final stage of the County Cup. Great Danton may be the outsiders, but a victory over

77

Medville by at least two clear goals would see them snatch the title on goal difference – so long as the College and Lakeview only draw with one another. Each team's goal difference (GD) is calculated by subtracting their goals against figure from the goals for, perhaps resulting in a negative number! While we're doing a spot of maths, you might even like to work out some other possible permutations, based on the final two fixtures:

Lakeview v Needham College
Great Danton v Medville Comprehensive

Leading Cup scorers
2 – **Bridges** (Medville); **Mistry** (Lakeview)

WOMEN'S FOOTBALL

. . . it's the boys' turn to watch their teacher play football – and Joe takes cousin Harry to meet Miss Jackson . . .

'Great tackle, Jacko!' cried Joe from the grand-stand.

'Quiet, you nutter!' hissed Ben, the Lakeview captain.

'She won't know it's me. There's loads of other people shouting stuff.'

The boys were sitting with Ben's dad in the main stand of Medville Town F.C. watching the floodlit cup game between Medville Ladies and Shelthorpe Ladies from the South Quarter. The local team were leading 2–0 and Ruth Jackson was having an outstanding game in Joe's own position at right wing-back.

'Ouch! I bet that hurt,' said Joe in admiration as their teacher sent her opponent crashing to the ground. 'Jacko tackles harder than me.'

'Anybody tackles harder than you,' scoffed Harry.

'Watch it!'

'What do you think about our Jacko, Harry?' asked Ben.

'Good player, by the look of it,' he replied and then grinned. 'Got better legs than old Yardley as well. He's not a pretty sight in shorts!'

'Jacko had better not hear you say that kind of thing about her,' chuckled Ben. 'She doesn't like any sexist comments.'

Medville's third goal was a classic. Jacko over-lapped down the right wing, beat a defender with a pacy dribble and then hooked over a high cross for the number ten to send a bullet header into the net.

The final score was 3–0 and the boys joined other spectators on the pitch to congratulate the players as they left the field.

'Can I have your autograph, please?' Joe called out.

The Medville number four turned round and grinned. 'You cheeky monkey, Joe Vernon. I'd recognize that voice anywhere.'

'Told you we were coming to watch tonight, miss.'

'I thought you were kidding me. So where's your autograph book?'

'Er, I haven't got one, miss, sorry. You could sign my maths book at school tomorrow, if you like.'

'I don't think that would really be a good idea,' she said, before turning to the boy next to him. 'And I guess you must be Harry. I saw your picture in the paper.'

'Who didn't?' laughed Ben. 'He even got his mug on the telly.'

Harry reddened. 'Yes, sorry about all that fuss,' he murmured. 'I don't make a habit of doing stupid things like running off.'

'I'm glad to hear it,' she smiled. 'If I choose somebody to play in a match, I expect him to be there.'

'He's starting at Lakeview on Monday,' said Joe.

'So I gather,' replied the teacher. 'Well, you'd better come along to our next practice, then, Harry, and show me what you can do.'

'He can be our new signing to replace Ravi,' put in Ben.

'One good thing about missing that local derby,' said Harry sheepishly. 'At least it means I'm not cup-tied!'

LAKEVIEW v NEEDHAM COLLEGE

Saturday 29 November
k.o. 10 a.m.
Referee: Mr J. Underwood

. . . a crucial game for both schools: victory would lift them to the top of the group table – but defeat or a draw means exit from the County Cup . . .

'Blimey, look!' gasped Ben as he pulled on his boots outside the changing room. 'Underwood must be the ref.'

It was the first time that the Lakeview footballers had seen their headteacher in a tracksuit. But the captain had failed to notice Miss Jackson standing behind him.

'Ahem!' she coughed. 'That's *Mister* Underwood to you, Ben Thorpe. He happened to be a P.E. teacher once, just like me. He offered to referee this morning so that I'm free to shout at you lot from the touchline.'

Mr O'Donald already had the College team out on the pitch, warming up. 'Good luck, lads,' he said. 'You've beaten them in the league,

83

remember, so go and do it again today. Give it everything you've got.'

It was the College captain, Jayesh, who had the first shot of the game. The overnight rain had made the surface greasy and the ball skidded through the goal-keeper's hands to thump into his chest before he held on tight.

'Saved, Elvis!' shouted Ben.

Miss Jackson echoed the praise. 'Well done. Good job you got your body right behind that one.'

Elvis threw the ball out as usual and found his left wing-back, Dan, who swapped passes with Ben to create space for Jaspal Singh to run at goal. Jaspal may have been wearing Ravi's number ten shirt, but he wasn't such a reliable finisher. He sliced the ball well wide of the target.

Chances continued to go begging at both ends, with players struggling to keep their feet in the slippery conditions as the rain began again. It was a surprise that only one goal was scored before the interval. The Lakeview captain made the breakthrough, but most of the credit was due to Dan for another dash up the left wing. He left muddy white shirts trailing in his wake before pulling the ball back into Ben's path for him to fire home.

Miss Jackson could be hard to please. The coach made it plain during her half-time team talk that she wasn't happy with their overall performance. 'We're still not fizzing that ball around like we should,' she pointed out. 'Pass and move, pass and move, OK?'

'Mr Underwood won't abandon the game, will he, miss, if this rain keeps up?' asked Ben anxiously.

'Not unless it gets *really* bad – and especially if we've still got our noses in front!' she said with a grin. 'But, remember, goal difference could be vital in a tight group like this. One goal might not be enough.'

The College knew they had to go all out for goals too. Tom Wright had remained out of favour – and out of the team – since the incident in the Great Danton game, but Mr O'Donald turned to the substitute now as a proven goalscorer. It was a risky strategy, making his side top heavy with attackers, but the teacher calculated that this was the time to gamble.

Playing only three at the back, College surged forward from the kick-off like a cavalry charge. The ball was switched from one side of the pitch to the other and when right-winger Kyle's shot was blocked, Tom's first touch sent the rebound ballooning over the bar.

'Unlucky!' shouted Mr O'Donald. 'That's more like it, College. Keep it up. Play the game in their half.'

The rain was driving into the faces of the Lakeview defenders and they needed all the help they could get from their midfield teammates. Ben found himself having to play as a kind of emergency sweeper, trying to break up the visitors' attacks before they could get in a shot. All good intentions about slick passing were forgotten. They were content at times simply to boot the ball away anywhere just to relieve the pressure.

Miss Jackson decided that reinforcements were required. She turned to her substitutes and told Harry and Nathan Finch to get ready to come on. 'We need some fresh legs and cool heads in defence. Have you got a cool head, Harry?'

'It's freezing, miss,' he grinned, thrilled to be

making his début for his new school.

'Good, so use it,' she laughed. 'Tell the others not to panic as well. Whenever we just whack it upfield, it's coming straight back at us.'

As she spoke, College forced a corner and Callum ran forward to add his height to the attack. Lakeview recognized the danger, but could do nothing to stop the big defender soaring high to meet the cross. Elvis came to the rescue, stretching to tip the header behind for yet another corner.

Left-winger Paul surprised Lakeview with a different tactic, screwing the ball low across the area instead of aiming for Callum's head. It ricocheted among the crowd of players as if in a pinball machine until it spun to the feet of Champagne. Unfortunately, he got them in a tangle and with the goal at his mercy, his standing foot slipped in the mud and the hero of College's previous Cup win scooped the ball wide.

'I don't believe it!' cried Mr O'Donald in anguish. 'How could he miss?'

Jayesh pulled Champagne up. 'Can't be helped,' he said generously, 'but I don't think you'll be getting ten out of ten again now.'

After the Lakeview substitutions were made,

Nathan's first contribution to the game was to foul Tom on the edge of the penalty area. 'Direct free-kick,' announced the referee and Tom glanced hopefully at his captain.

'All right, you take it,' said Jayesh. 'Let's have one of your specials.'

Lakeview had all ten outfield players back to defend, with a five-man wall bracing themselves for Tom's expected cannonball. Jaspal was the human brick that took the full force of the impact, and he crumpled to the ground in pain as Joe hoofed the ball out of play.

The corner was delayed while Jaspal redis-covered how to breathe, but it was only a brief respite. When the ball swirled over into the penalty area, Callum rose above all the other players and this time Elvis was beaten. The header was placed beyond his reach, but Nathan was guarding the post and made amends by hacking the ball away. The clearance did not go very far. Mark Jewell was lurking on the edge of the area and he was just lining himself up for a strike at goal when Harry whipped the ball off his toes.

'Out! Out!' screamed Elvis.

There was no-one yet for Harry to pass to, so he kept possession by dribbling the ball towards the touchline to allow his teammates to stream out of defence. College were caught on the break, hopelessly outnumbered.

Harry's well-timed pass was lethal.

Looking up, he spotted Henry galloping through the middle, played onside by a single defender, and he released the ball perfectly into the number nine's path. Henry worked the ball on to his stronger right foot, evading a lunging tackle, and then let fly.

D.J. didn't stand a chance. The goalkeeper's dive was only a token effort at making a save. It was like waving the ball goodbye as it sped past him. He might also have been waving a sad farewell to his team's ambitions in the County Cup. College were now 2–0 down and they couldn't even hope to be saved by the weather. The rain had suddenly stopped as if the football gods had turned off the giant sprinkler in the sky.

As soon as Mr Underwood blew the final whistle, Elvis ran up to Harry and slapped him on the back, leaving a dirty stain on the newcomer's shirt. The delighted keeper might have been caked in mud, but he had still somehow managed to keep a clean sheet.

'Well played,' he said. 'You might win a regular place in the team now, Harry.'

'Hope so. It's just great to feel wanted, that's the main thing.'

Joe butted in. 'Yeah, but not as good a feeling as being top of the table!'

Result:	Lakeview 2 v 0 Needham College
	h-t: 1 – 0
Scorers:	Thorpe
	Tudor

WHAT IF?

... take a look at the latest group table printed in the Medville Mail *newspaper – Mr Yardley has pinned a copy of it on the Year 7 noticeboard at the Comp, knowing that the sight of local rivals Lakeview above them will be all the motivation his players will need for their last Cup game ...*

GROUP TABLE

	P	W	D	L	Goals F	Goals A	(GD)	Pts
Lakeview	3	1	2	0	5	3	(+2)	5
Medville	2	1	1	0	5	3	(+2)	4
Needham College	3	1	0	2	3	6	(−3)	3
Great Danton	2	0	1	1	2	3	(−1)	1

'There's nothing Lakeview can do now to stop us winning the Quarter Shield,' said Skinny, the Comp's right-back, studying the table with some of his teammates at lunchtime. 'They'll just have to sweat it out.'

'Nobody's gonna stop us winning it,' Ryan stated confidently.

'Well, apart from Great Danton of course.'

The captain gave a snort. 'Danton aren't great, they're rubbish!'

'And they've got nothing to play for now they can't qualify themselves,' added Monty, throwing his empty crisps packet on to the floor. 'Bet they won't really be trying all that hard.'

'Hope not,' said Adam, 'but it won't just be a walkover. They've got a few good players, y'know, like Q and Chris Vaughan. And their keeper, what's-his-name, isn't bad either.'

'Nidesh,' said Ryan. 'He's been in the area squad a couple of times. Can't get a game of course 'cos of me. I'm so brilliant!'

They all laughed, but only Monty dared to have a little dig at the captain. 'No wonder you're hard to beat in goal – your head fills most of it!'

Ryan shot his pal a dirty look. 'Anyway, like I said, we're gonna thrash Danton on Saturday and make Lakeview pig-sick – including Harry Glenn. That'll make him wish he'd never deserted us.'

'Even just a draw will do,' said Skinny. 'I mean, we'll still have the same goal difference as Lakeview, but we'd go top 'cos we would've scored more goals than them.'

'Not if it's nil–nil, we won't,' Adam pointed out. 'Everything would be exactly the same then.'

'No chance!' Ryan sneered. 'Goal-less draws at our age are about as rare as Monty offering us any of his crisps.'

'Yeah, but what if it did work out like that?' Adam persisted. 'I'd hate to lose out to Lakeview on a toss of a coin or something.'

The footballers were appalled at such a thought. It even made Ryan forget about Monty's jibe at him. 'Nah, the title wouldn't be decided in that kind of way . . .' he said, shaking his head, ' . . . would it?'

'C'mon, guys, let's go and find Yardley,' said Monty in alarm. 'We've gotta know for sure what might happen – just in case . . .'

. . . the Lakeview players already know the score, so to speak, but some of them can't wait to learn their fate – Miss Jackson is taking a carload of boys to Great Danton to see which Medville school will be able to claim the Quarter Shield . . .

GREAT DANTON v MEDVILLE

Saturday 6 December
k.o. 10 a.m.
Referee: Mr B. Goddard

. . . deep into the second half, it's still 0–0 and the hopes of the watching Lakeview party are rising with every minute – and then there's a penalty! . . .

'Yes!' cried Joe. 'Well spotted, ref. Good decision.'

'What happened?' demanded Harry, starting to run with his teammates to get behind the goal. 'I didn't see anything.'

'Good job the ref did. Definite handball.'

The Comp players didn't think so at all. 'Accidental, ref,' protested Monty. 'The ball just hit my hand.'

Mr Goddard waved him away. 'It prevented a goalscoring opportunity,' he said sternly. 'Penalty.'

The players looked over to their own teacher for support, but there was nothing that Mr Yardley could do. 'Just save it, Ryan,' he shouted angrily. 'They don't deserve to score.'

The referee shooed all the excited spectators from around the goal. 'Stand well away, lads,' he told them. 'I don't want anybody distracted.'

'We do,' Ben muttered to Elvis. 'Especially Ryan.'

'Yeah, if he doesn't save this, we'll be champions.'

The Lakeview captain shook his head. 'Maybe not. If the Comp went and equalized, we'd be worse off then, remember. They'd have scored one more goal than us.'

Miss Jackson had explained the situation again in the car as they drove to the game. Unless the Comp actually lost, the only result Lakeview could hope for would be a 0–0 draw to leave the two teams tied at the top of the table. And that would mean a head-to-head play-off sometime to decide who went through to the semi-finals of the County Cup.

'The trouble is,' the teacher added, 'there hasn't been a goal-less game in the Cup apparently for about three seasons.'

'Come on, *please* score,' Harry urged fervently as the kicker placed the ball on the penalty spot. 'I couldn't bear a play-off against the Comp.'

Sam Isherwood wiped a piece of mud from the

end of his right boot, deliberately not looking at the goalkeeper who was jumping up and down on his line.

'You're gonna miss,' Ryan called out to him. 'I'm the penalty king.'

'Shut that big-head up, Ishy,' urged Chris, the Great Danton captain. 'He's a real pain.'

Mr Goddard blew the whistle and Ishy ran in. From the direction of the angled run-up, Ryan guessed where the ball might go and threw himself to his left.

It was an inspired guess. Ryan not only got his hands to the ball but even succeeded in clinging on to it.

As cheers and groans echoed around the school playing fields, Ryan was mobbed by his teammates. He savoured the moment, keeping the ball tightly hugged to his chest while basking in their praise.

'C'mon, we can still win this game, guys,' he cried. 'Get up there and stick this ball in the back of their net.'

He kicked it away up the sloping pitch and then turned to leer at the disappointed Lakeview players. 'Stuff you lot,' he cackled. 'They're not gonna get the ball past me today.'

There was not very much they could say in reply and they trailed back around the touchline to where Miss Jackson was standing.

'Great save of Ryan's,' said Joe generously. 'Have to give him that.'

Harry pulled a face. 'Yeah, but don't tell him.'

'No need,' Joe sighed. 'I reckon he already knows.'

'Pity about that,' said Miss Jackson. 'I really can't see anybody scoring now. Both teams have struggled to play uphill into the wind.'

That had certainly been the case for the home side before half-time and now the visitors were finding the same problem. Playing in their change-strip of all-yellow because of a colour

97

clash, the Comp had barely managed a shot on target. When they did, they found Nidesh in fine form.

The keeper made his best save of the match just five minutes from the end. Adam's far-post header from Skinny's cross looked destined for the top corner of the goal until Nidesh leapt to his right to pluck it out of the air. Miss Jackson let out an involuntary squeal of relief, which made all her players laugh. It showed them how much the Cup meant to her too.

'Well saved, keeper!' she called out.

'Almost as good as one of mine,' put in Elvis.

'Phew! We nearly had it there, didn't we, miss,' said Ben. 'You keep telling us the game isn't over till the final whistle.'

That old saying was proved true yet again. In the dying seconds, Chris broke through up the left for Great Danton and found Ishy with a lofted pass. The attacker headed it down for leading scorer Q to strike, but his volley was bravely blocked by a defender. Ishy pounced on the rebound, held off Skinny's challenge and then hooked the ball at goal with his weaker left foot.

Had Ishy made clean contact, Ryan was well positioned to make the save, but the keeper was wrong-footed by the sliced shot. The ball looped beyond his reach and bobbled agonizingly goal-wards as Paramjit chased back and stretched out a long leg in desperation . . .

'I don't believe it!' cried Harry.

. . . what's happened? Is Harry going to have to suffer a play-off against his old school or not? . . .

POSTSCRIPT

. . . it's time now for the after-match presentation ceremony and two boys are about to step up to receive the Quarter Shield . . .

'I could kill him!' Harry muttered to his cousin out of the corner of his mouth.

'Who?'

'Who d'yer think? Pram-Man, of course. For kicking the ball off the line like that right at the end.'

'Yeah, I think I'll help you do it,' Joe said with a sigh. 'If your pal hadn't got in the way, the Comp would have lost and we'd have been Quarter Champions on our own – instead of having to share the title with that mob.'

'And have to meet them in a play-off to see who goes through to the semis,' Harry added gloomily. 'That's about the last thing I wanted.'

'Did Yardley speak to you today?'

Harry nodded. 'Yeah, briefly, as he passed me once.'

'What did he say?'

'Hello, Glenn, how are you?'

They chuckled and then joined in the applause as both Ben and Ryan walked forward to collect the Shield from the local organizer of the Cup competition. Somewhat awkwardly, the two winning captains held up the large trophy between them as more cheers rang out from the spectators. Then they caught one another's eye and tightened their grip on the Shield. Neither of them wanted to let go of it again.

'OK, lads, no need to have a tug-of-war with it,' the man laughed, trying to make a joke of their little tussle to the crowd. 'As joint Champions, Medville Comprehensive and Lakeview High will each keep the Shield for six months.'

'As the Comp are already the holders, we'll have it first,' said Ryan.

'That's not fair,' claimed Ben. 'It should be our turn now.'

'Um, I think the best way to settle this will be to toss for it, don't you?' the organizer decided, fumbling for a coin in his pocket. 'Heads, the Comp – tails, Lakeview, OK?'

He flipped the coin high into the air. Many pairs of eyes strained to see the outcome as it hit the ground and rolled before flopping over on to one side. They really didn't need to bother. Ryan suddenly gave  a loud whoop and snatched the Shield out of Ben's grasp at the same time.

'Huh! Typical of Ryan's luck, that is,' said Harry in disgust, watching the Comp players celebrate the minor triumph over their rivals.

'Well, guess we'll just have to change his luck in the play-off, won't we?' Joe grinned. 'Jacko said there won't be time to arrange the match before the end of term so it'll have to wait now till after Christmas.'

'Oh, great!' Harry murmured sarcastically under his breath. 'That'll give me something to look forward to during the holidays.'

Ryan could not resist a final jibe at Ben. 'This Shield is going straight back in the Comp's trophy cabinet – where it belongs,' he smirked.

'Only on loan – make sure you keep it polished for us,' Ben retorted. 'We'll have won the County Cup by then so they'll look nice together in ours.'

'Rubbish! We're gonna thrash you in the play-off,' Ryan snarled. 'I'm almost glad it's turned out like this.'

'How d'yer mean?'

'Cos it gives us the chance to prove who's really the best team in town!'

. . . so who do you reckon that will be? Looks like we'll all have to wait until the New Year to find out what happens in the play-off, but it's sure to be a crunch game – in more ways than one.

Don't miss it! Read about the big clash in book 5 of the series . . .

APPENDIX

RESULTS

Gt Danton	1 v 1	Lakeview
Medville	3 v 1	College
Lakeview	2 v 2	Medville
College	2 v 1	Gt Danton
Lakeview	2 v 0	College
Gt Danton	0 v 0	Medville

FINAL GROUP TABLE

	P	W	D	L	F	A	(GD)	Pts
Lakeview	3	1	2	0	5	3	(+2)	5
Medville	3	1	2	0	5	3	(+2)	5
Needham College	3	1	0	2	3	6	(−3)	3
Great Danton	3	0	2	1	2	3	(−1)	2

The two unbeaten schools, Lakeview High and Medville Comprehensive, are tied at the top of the table, equal on points, goal difference and goals scored. As joint East Quarter Champions, there will now be a play-off match between them to decide which team will qualify for the two-legged, semi-final stage of the County Cup.

GOALS

A total of 15 goals were scored in the six group games, averaging just 2.5 per match. These were the goalscorers for each school:

GREAT DANTON

1 – Quinn, Woods

LAKEVIEW

2 – Mistry
1 – Vernon, Thorpe, Tudor

MEDVILLE

2 – Bridges
1 – Joyner, Montgomery, Yorke

NEEDHAM COLLEGE

1 – Wright, Parmar, Cork

ABOUT THE AUTHOR

Rob Childs was born and grew up in Derby. His childhood ambition was to become an England cricketer or footballer – preferably both! After university, however, he went into teaching and taught in primary and high schools in Leicestershire, where he now lives. Always interested in school sports, he coached school teams and clubs across a range of sports, and ran area representative teams in football, cricket and athletics.

Recognizing a need for sports fiction for young readers, he decided to have a go at writing such stories himself and now has more than fifty books to his name, including the popular *The Big Match* series, published by Young Corgi Books.

Rob has now left teaching in order to be able to write full-time. Married to Joy, also a writer, Rob has a 'lassie' dog called Laddie and is also a keen photographer.

Who else will qualify for the semi-finals of the County
Cup? Read the other books in the series and find out!

THE COUNTY CUP
1. CUP FAVOURITES
Rob Childs

Quarter-Finals

Four schools are competing for the North Quarter
Shield and a place in the semi-finals of the County
Cup – the trophy every player wants to win!

Who will be the Champions of the North?

Foxgrove High School
The favourites, known as the 'Foxes', are on the scent
of the Shield again...

Glendale Community School
An attacking team with a Giant striker – but with a
mean streak in midfield...

Market Bagley Community School
Playing a sweeper system, the Baggies are in for some
Ding-Dong battles...

Teffield Community School
Group outsiders perhaps, but playing at full volume...

Join the Cup trail and enjoy all the drama – on and
off the pitch – in this action-packed series from Rob
Childs, author of the bestselling *Soccer Mad* books.

0 440 86383X

THE COUNTY CUP
3. CUP SHOCKS
Rob Childs

Quarter-Finals.

Four schools are competing for the South Quarter Shield and a place in the semi-finals of the County Cup – the trophy every player wants to win!

Who will be Champions of the South?

Fyleden Community College: group underdogs on paper, but they hope to bite back on the pitch...

Oakfield High School: red-hot in attack, they're out to set a new Cup goalscoring record...

Shelthorpe Comprehensive School: last season's Cup-winners are desperate to keep it in their trophy cabinet...

St Wystan's Comprehensive School: the captain's keen to log some victories to help the Saints go marching on...

Join the Cup trail and enjoy the drama – on and off the pitch – in this action-packed series from Rob Childs, author of the bestselling *Soccer Mad* books.

0 440 863856

COUNTY CUP
4. CUP CLASHES
Rob Childs

Quarter-Finals

Four schools are competing for the West Quarter Shield and a place in the semi-finals of the County Cup – the trophy every player wants to win!

Who will be the Champions of the West?

Hillcrest Comprehensive School: out to show their teacher that the 'good old days' are back...

Kingsway Green High School: hoping a dash of foreign flair will keep them on the soccer map...

Riverside Comprehensive School: a team of high flyers, wanting to win and feel over the Moon...

Westbridge Community College: it's not only their waterlogged pitches that tend to cut up rough...

Join the Cup trail and enjoy the drama – on and off the pitch – in this action-packed series from Rob Childs, author of the bestselling *Soccer Mad* books.

0 440 863864

All Transworld titles are available by post from:

**Book Service By Post, PO Box 29,
Douglas, Isle of Man, IM99 1BQ**

Credit cards accepted. Please telephone 01624 675137,
fax 01624 670923 or Internet http://www.bookpost.co.uk
or e-mail: bookshop@enterprise.net for details

Free postage and packing in the UK. Overseas customers:
allow £1 per book (paperbacks) and £3 per book (hardbacks)

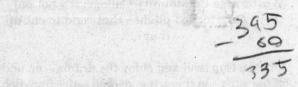